Welcome

The New Kid

Like how a frown turned upside down becomes a smile,

this story could have a happy ending!

Did you know that

there's another way to treat the new kid?

Why would you think

they don't belong at our school?

Guess what?

It's fun to make new friends and learn things from them.

Some kids say,

"We don't want anyone else in our group.

Pretend we don't see them!"

I have a better idea. Let's

share our table and snacks.

The new kid can't
go find another school.
Let's tell them,
"Welcome!"

They're not
so different from me—and my friends.

Check out the new kid.

Seriously?

Would you like to be that lonely kid?

If your family moved near a different school, how would you feel?

I've heard people say,

"Why do *I* have to be nice to the new kid?"

I mean,

it

is

easy to say hi to someone new,

isn't

it?

The New Kid Welcome

It
isn't
easy to say hi to someone new,
is
it?
I mean,
why do *I* have to be nice to the new kid?

I've heard people say,
"How would you feel
if your family moved near a different school?
Would you like to be that lonely kid?"
Seriously?!
Check them out.
So different from me—and my friends.

They're not
welcome.
Let's tell them,
"Go find another school!"
The new kid can't
share our table and snacks.
I have a better idea. Let's
pretend we don't see them.

We don't want anyone else in our group.
Some kids say,
"It's fun to make new friends and learn things from them."
Guess what?
They don't belong at our school!
Why would you think
there's another way to treat the new kid?

Did you know that
this story could have a happy ending?
Like how a frown turned upside down becomes a smile.

Welcome The New Kid

Like how a frown turned upside down becomes a smile,
this story could have a happy ending!
Did you know that
there's another way to treat the new kid?
Why would you think
they don't belong at our school?
Guess what?
It's fun to make new friends and learn things from them.

Some kids say,
"We don't want anyone else in our group.
Pretend we don't see them!"
I have a better idea. Let's
share our table and snacks.

The new kid can't
go find another school.
Let's tell them,
"Welcome!"
They're not
so different from me—and my friends.
Check them out.

Seriously?
Would you like to be that lonely kid?
If your family moved near a different school,
how would you feel?

I've heard people say,
"Why do *I* have to be nice to the new kid?"
I mean,
it
is
easy to say hi to someone new,
isn't
it?

. . . turn this story upside down and read it backward!

Did you know that

this story could have a happy ending?

Like how a frown turned upside down becomes a smile . . .

Why would you think
there's another way to treat the new kid?

We don't want anyone else in our group.

Some kids say,

"It's fun to make new friends and learn things from them."

Guess what?

They don't belong at our school!

They're not
welcome.
Let's tell them,
"Go find another school!"
The new kid can't
share our table and snacks.
I have a better idea. Let's
pretend we don't see them.

I've heard people say,

"How would you feel

if your family moved near a different school?

Would you like to be that lonely kid?"

Seriously?!

Check out the new kid.

So different from me—and my friends.

It
isn't
easy to say hi to someone new,
is
it?
I mean,
why do *I* have to be nice to the new kid?

There's another side
to this story!

The New Kid
Welcome

by
Suzanne Slade

illustrated by
Nicole Miles

Rodale Kids RODALE KiDS New York

To Mark, Erik, and Ava
—S.S.

To Mum, Dad, Dylan, and Dan
—N.M.

Text copyright © 2022 by Suzanne Slade
Jacket art and interior illustrations copyright © 2022 by Nicole Miles

All rights reserved. Published in the United States by Rodale Kids, an imprint of
Random House Children's Books, a division of Penguin Random House LLC, New York.

Rodale and the colophon are registered trademarks and
Rodale Kids is a trademark of Penguin Random House LLC.

Visit us on the Web! rhcbooks.com

Educators and librarians, for a variety of teaching tools, visit us at RHTeachersLibrarians.com

Library of Congress Cataloging-in-Publication Data is available upon request.
ISBN 978-0-593-42632-6 (hardcover) — ISBN 978-0-593-42633-3 (lib. bdg.) —
ISBN 978-0-593-42634-0 (ebook)

The artist created the illustrations for this book digitally.
The text of this book is set in 15-point Mikado.
Interior design by Taline Boghosian

MANUFACTURED IN CHINA   10 9 8 7 6 5 4 3 2 1   First Edition